P9-CQR-846

For Calder, Mabel, and Jonathan —A.G.

Farrar Straus Giroux Books for Young Readers
An imprint of Macmillan Publishing Group, LLC
175 Fifth Avenue, New York, NY 10010

Text copyright © 2017 by Alison Goldberg
Pictures copyright © 2017 by Mike Yamada
All rights reserved
Color separations by Embassy Graphics
Printed in China by RR Donnelley Asia Printing Solutions Ltd.,
Dongguan City, Guangdong Province
Designed by Kristie Radwilowicz
First edition, 2017
10 9 8 7 6 5 4 3 2 1

mackids.com

Library of Congress Cataloging-in-Publication Data

Names: Goldberg, Alison, author. | Yamada, Mike, illustrator.
Title: I love you for miles and miles / Alison Goldberg ; pictures by Mike
    Yamada.
Description: First edition. | New York : Farrar Straus Giroux, 2017. |
    Summary: Describes the depth, height, and steadiness of one's love for
    another by comparing it with the deepest drill, tallest crane, and
    steadiest tugboat.
Identifiers: LCCN 2016058781 | ISBN 9780374304430 (hardcover)
Subjects: | CYAC: Love—Fiction. | Trucks—Fiction. | Vehicles—Fiction.
Classification: LCC PZ7.1.G626 Iaae 2017 | DDC [E]—dc23
LC record available at https://lccn.loc.gov/2016058781

Our books may be purchased in bulk for promotional, educational, or business use.
Please contact your local bookseller or the Macmillan Corporate and Premium Sales Department
at (800) 221-7945 ext. 5442 or by e-mail at MacmillanSpecialMarkets@macmillan.com.

I LOVE YOU
FOR Miles AND Miles

ALISON GOLDBERG   **PICTURES BY MIKE YAMADA**

Farrar Straus Giroux • New York

My love for you is
Longer than the longest train
Linking engine to caboose,
Winding for miles and miles.

My love for you is
Wider than the widest big rig
Stretching side to side,
Hauling loads of every shape and size.

My love for you is
Stronger than the strongest excavator
Scooping heap after heap,
Lifting with a mighty arm.

My love for you is
Deeper than the deepest drill
Digging down, down, down,
Uncovering mysteries.

My love for you is
Taller than the tallest crane
Rising up, up, up,
Reaching toward the sun.

My love for you is
Smoother than the smoothest sailboat
Skimming wave after wave,
Gliding along.

My love for you is
Faster than the fastest fire truck
Hurrying faster, faster,
Rushing to you, anywhere you are.

My love for you is
Tougher than the toughest tractor
Planting crop after crop,
Helping through mud and muck.

My love for you is
Bigger than the biggest truck
Removing boulders and rocks,
Clearing the way.

My love for you is
Higher than the highest plane
Flying higher, higher,
Soaring above all the rain.

My love for you is
Steadier than the steadiest tugboat
Tugging *puff, puff, puff,*
Guiding you home, day or night.

My love for you is
Longer than the longest train
Riding from station to station,
Traveling with you always.